A DAY WITH Wilbur Robinson

by
WILLIAM JOYCE

A DAY WITH

Wilbur Robinson

by

WILLIAM JOYCE

LAURA GERINGER BOOKS
An Imprint of HarperCollinsPublishers

I'd like you to meet the Robinsons.

Wilbur Robinson is my best friend, and his house

is the *greatest* place to visit.

i walked up and said hello to the twin uncles, Dmitri and Spike. As always, Wilbur opened the door just before I knocked.

"Come on in," he said. "Lefty will take your bag."

I t's kind of dull around here today," said Wilbur.

I looked around. Aunt Billie was playing with her train set, Cousin Pete was walking the cats, and Uncle Gaston sat comfortably in the family cannon.

"Your dad needs you out in the backyard," he shouted as he blasted himself across the room.

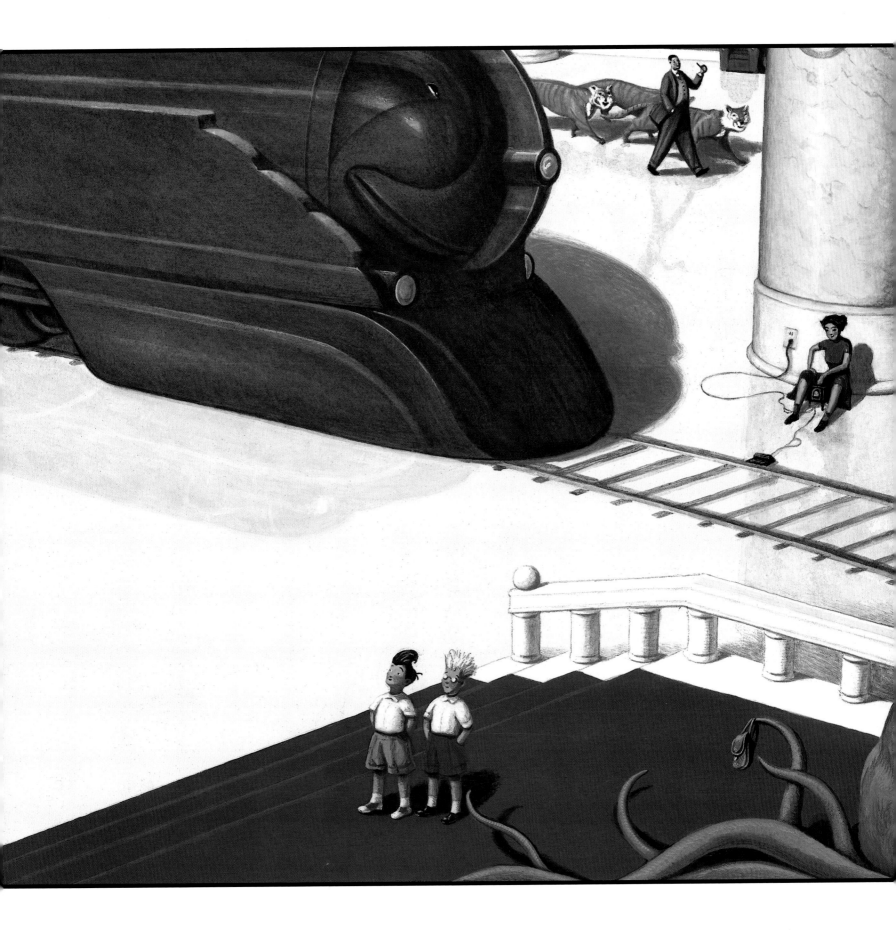

In the backyard, we found Mr. and Mrs. Robinson and their robot, Carl. They were scouring the lawn with the matter detector.

"We're looking for Grandfather's false teeth," Mr. Robinson explained. "Of course, we haven't seen *Grandfather* lately either," he added. "Could you boys go and ask around?"

We asked Uncle Wormly if he'd seen Grandfather's teeth, but he was busy with a new friend. One of his bugs suggested we check out back. The photon elevator was busted, so we took the stairs.

"I don't remember the weather report mentioning snow for the east wing," yelped Wilbur.

After helping Uncle Nimbus with his new snowball shooting device, we searched on but found neither Grandfather nor his teeth.

None of the lab equipment had seen a thing. But Uncle Orbley popped by to lend a hand.

"Ask Uncle Judlow," he gurgled. "He knows everything!"

We found Uncle Judlow, relaxing with his brain augmentor.

"It helps him think deep thoughts," Wilbur whispered.

"Mississippi spelled with *o*'s instead of *i*'s would be *Mossossoppo*!" blurted Uncle Judlow.

"See? What did I tell you?" Wilbur exclaimed.

"Have you seen Grandfather Robinson's false teeth?" I asked.

Uncle Judlow blinked. "They're wherever he left them," he answered after some thought.

In the den, Wilbur's sister Tallulah was talking on the phone and eating grapes. His other sister, Blanche, was modeling her new prom dress.

"Do the shoes match?" she asked.

"They're swell," we chimed.

"Have you seen Grandfather Robinson's false teeth?" I asked.

"Or Grandfather?" asked Wilbur.

"Not lately," said Blanche.

Yawning, Tallulah shook her head and ate another grape.

Somebody had left the Time Machine on, so the dinosaurs were at their usual spot by the pool.

"Jeez, I hope Grandfather didn't get lost in the Mesozoic period again," said Wilbur.

"That'll definitely make him late for dinner," I said.

We're striking out," said Wilbur, discouraged. "And I'm hungry, so let's eat."

Cousin Laszlo came by to demonstrate his new antigravity device.

"Have you seen Grandfather Robinson's false teeth?" I asked.

"Nope, but I bet they're floating around here someplace," mused Cousin Laszlo.

Suddenly the faint familiar strains of "Potato Head Blues" came wafting from the house.

That's it!" yelled Wilbur. "It's Friday—Grandfather's in his lab working with his dancing frog band!"

We rushed to the lab. Sure enough, there was Grandfather with his friends Mr. Ellington and Mr. Armstrong. Grandmother Robinson was helping.

"Have you found your teeth, Grandfather?" shouted Wilbur over the music.

"Nah, haven't theen 'em." He smiled.

"I guess we'll just keep looking," I volunteered.

"Thure do apprethiate it," said Grandfather as the music played on.

II

We found Grandfather!" Wilbur announced as we ran outside.

"Good work!" said Mr. Robinson. "Now if we could only find those teeth!"

"Last time I was here, we were looking for your grandfather's glass eye," I reminded Wilbur as we walked.

"Yeah, he's always missing a part," Wilbur admitted.

"Ahoy!" called Uncle Art, newly arrived from abroad. "Looking for a lost bit of Grandfather? Gadzooks, I've been homesick."

by evening,
Grandfather's teeth were
still nowhere to be found.

At dinner, Uncle
Gaston practiced shooting
food out of a cannon.
Carl and Lefty served
while Grandfather did the
best he could without his
teeth.

after dinner, Mrs. Robinson read *Tarzan of the Apes* aloud. Suddenly, one of the frogs jumped up onto my hand and did a Tarzan yodel. *He was wearing Grandfather Robinson's teeth.*

"I found them! I found them!" I cried.

Everybody shouted, "Hooray!" except for Wilbur, who did a Tarzan yodel too.

the occasion called for a pillow fight.

xhausted from the battle, we floated across the lawn and into a tree with the help of Cousin Laszlo's antigravity device. Wilbur and I stayed up late into the night while Uncle Art told hair-raising stories about his adventures in outer space, as the frogs played softly on their violins.

The next morning, the whole family gathered to wave good-bye, singing "Yes, We Have No Bananas," just like they always do.

I was kind of sad to leave, but I was ready to go home for a while.

"Good-bye, Wilbur," I said.

"Sorry it was such a dull day," Wilbur apologized.

"Hey, I had fun," I said. Wilbur smiled.

he sun was shining brightly as I walked slowly away. I looked back over my shoulder, and there was Wilbur, shooting himself out of Uncle Gaston's cannon with a farewell message:

For John Henderson Cade—
a matchless pal and Robinson to the core.
—W.J.

A Day with Wilbur Robinson
Copyright © 1990, 2006 by William Joyce
Manufactured in China. All rights reserved. No part of this book may be used or
reproduced in any manner whatsoever without written permission except in the case of brief quotations
embodied in critical articles and reviews. For information address HarperCollins Children's Books,
a division of HarperCollins Publishers, 10 East 53rd Street, New York, NY 10022.
www.harpercollinschildrens.com

Library of Congress Cataloging-in-Publication Data
Joyce, William, date
    A day with Wilbur Robinson / by William Joyce.
      p. cm.
    An expanded version of A day with Wilbur Robinson by the same author: New York : Harper
& Row, 1990.
    Summary: While spending the day in the Robinson household, Wilbur's best friend joins in
the search for Grandfather Robinson's missing false teeth and meets one wacky relative after another.
    ISBN-10: 0-06-089098-3 (trade bdg.) — ISBN-13: 978-0-06-089098-8 (trade bdg.)
    ISBN-10: 0-06-089099-1 (lib. bdg.) — ISBN-13: 978-0-06-089099-5 (lib. bdg.)
    [1. Eccentrics and eccentricities—Fiction. 2. Lost and found possessions—Fiction. 3. Humorous
stories.] I. Title.
PZ7.J857Mee 2006
[E]—dc22

2005037287
CIP
AC

Typography by Alicia Mikles ❖ 12 13 SCP 10 9 8 7 6 5 4